Gideon Elliot

Erotic Aggression

Gay BDSM Erotica

WARNING

This book contains sexually explicit scenes and adult language. It may be considered offensive to some readers. This book is for sale to adults ONLY.

Please store your files wisely where they cannot be accessed by underage readers.

* * * * * * * * * * * * * * * * * * *

WANT FREE COPIES OF MY BOOKS?
Just visit my blog and download free copies of my books:
http://gideon-elliot.awesomeauthors.org/gideon-elliot/

About the Publisher

4Fun Publishing, a member of **BLVNP Incorporated**, 340 S. Lemon #6200, Walnut CA 91789, info@blvnp.com / legal@blvnp.com
NOTE: Due to the highly emotional reaction of some people to works of erotic fiction, any email sent to the above address that contains foul language or religious references is automatically deleted by our anti-spam software and will not be seen. All other communications are welcome.

DISCLAIMER

Please don't be stupid and kill yourself. This book is a work of FICTION. Do not try any new sexual practice that you find in this book. It is fiction and not to be confused with reality. Neither the author nor the publisher or its associates assume any responsibility for any loss, injury, death or legal consequences resulting from acting on the contents in this book. Every character in this book is over 18 years of age. The author's opinions are not to be construed as the opinions of the publisher. The material in this book is for entertainment purposes ONLY. Enjoy.

Erotic Aggression
Gay BDSM Erotica

By: Gideon Elliot

ISBN: 978-1-62761-457-3

Chapter 1

It is a truism in this age, whose insights into human motivation have been shaped by the psychoanalytical hermeneutics that were introduced by the great Viennese physician, that great virtues are often the contrivances by means of which equally great vices present themselves as socially acceptable, without risking condemnation, and that, frequently, can bring upon their practitioner general approbation and enviable accolades.

Such it was with Martin Bower who from the earliest age found inordinate pleasure in the dismembering of small creatures while they still enjoyed, as it were, to have the breath of life throbbing in their diminutive corpuses. Plucking wings from flies and butterflies, and their thready legs from spiders, as his teeth clenched intent with the discharge of a rage that animated him, affected him with such personal excitement that it was never in the performance of these malicious surgeries but that the configurations of his countenance did not reveal the most intense and furious sympathetic sensibility with the creatures that were the objects of his mutilation.

Rather than being openly performed, these experiments in the assertion of power over nature were enacted secretly. The outward show the boy made as he grew into a handsome adolescent forecast nothing but grace, charm, and a deferential respect for others. This impression caused to be conferred upon him praise and admiration by all who could share in the responsibility for the quality of his growth and by all who were fortunate enough to observe in the young man the happy results of their efforts toward his education. At the age of thirteen he announced that he intended to be a surgeon when he grew up.

At University, his classmates admired him and his teachers esteemed him. He was recognized for intellectual brilliance and for emotional availability. His capacity to be compassionate, especially as he listened to stories whose narrators were rightfully angry, and his gratifying response to their tales with an uprush of anger, made him the first ear to turn to.

His first foray into cruelty lasted just under two years and he was done with it by the end of his junior year. Nor did it hamper the reputation for receptivity, availability, and affability, for genuine friendliness that made him shine -- in classes and in general on the campus. His devotion to cruelty was enacted in the odd recess each life can find, and it brought him into a parallel universe where he became someone else who was pretending to be him most of the time.

When he began at the University, Bower's father had given him an open-top two-seater car of a creamy pale Dresden green. The dashboard was of oak wood. The seats were of leather died a deep oxblood. In this car, from time to time, he left the campus and lonely along unlovely highways, he watched the road disappear beneath the car's wheels as he raced towards fulfillment of boundless desire.

He had discovered the club entirely by accident when he had gone to a remote village in search of the tranquility that a hamlet near a forest and a gently meandering stream can afford a young man of sensitivity and sensibility who is besieged by the excitements of an urban situation and a busy social routine intermixed, in his case, with an on-going course of rigorous studies, for his desire and determination to be a surgeon never wavered.

Hidden behind an imposing and antique stone wall that stretched along one side of a gently sloping dirt road across from the forest where he had wandered having left his car in a shaded and out-of-the-way grove, was a castle – at least a castle was what it most resembled – upon which he had stumbled some weeks ago because, as the day was hot, he had stripped off his clothes and, leaving them on the bank, plunged into the river and begun swimming with a strong and easy stroke until he had reached a turn in the river. It opened onto a prospect that gave him a surprising view of that marvelous stone structure, hidden, for the most part, by the wall he had seen from the road.

It would have been an event of no consequence had Bower seen the grave pile and having seen it turned round to return to the bank upon which he had left his clothes, and near which his convertible was parked. But circumstances greatly shaped by chance, a force whose origins are far from being transparent to the understanding, made it otherwise.

On the bank, quite close to the river, there composed into undeniable focus for the powerful swimmer a scene of even more commanding aspect than the edifice itself. It was of someone being beaten, whipped actually. The moment of his apprehension was also the moment of his response. Charging with a powerful stroke, he reached the shore and sprang out onto it from the river, oblivious to his own nakedness. He ran up to the scene of –it was not altercation, but attack, and cried, "Put down that whip. He is bleeding."

"And so will you be. Back off," cried at him the marvelous specimen of brawn brandishing the whip, his erection straining. But instead of backing off, Martin threw himself forward and, grabbing his opponent by one shoulder, yanked the whip out of his hand.

"What are you doing?" said the boy who lay in the tall grass bleeding, overwhelmed by the swollen masculinity that the naked man inhabited, and in awe.

Having interrupted something he thought he had been drawn to do as a courier of virtue, he soon became enmeshed in it to the full measure of his vice. Interrupted in their mystery, the participants were enraged and began together to pound the intruder in an embrace of blows, but with protean magnificence he slipped through their fingers and took his position before them with whip in hand, a naked circus master, as he cracked the whip on the earth before them and sent up clumps of dirt. Astonished, they held back and marveled. The whip was an extension of the arm that swung it, and danced in the same way that the muscles in the arms did.

"Who are you?" the one who no longer brandished the whip demanded as if still the master.

"I'd rather you answer that question regarding yourselves," Martin answered.

"You may not be happy if we do. You must come with us if you would know. But you've been warned."

The young man who had been beaten was hardly less naked than Martin, who let them guide him despite some wariness, keeping hold of the whip, as they walked, in front of him, to the castle. He wore only a black leather G-string; the straps of a leather harness crisscrossing his slim torso.

Inside Bower had to suppress a laugh.

"It surprises you," a young man, some five or seven years Martin's elder, inquired walking into the anteroom where Martin waited with the whipper – whom he had stripped of his whip – and the eager victim.

"No," Martin said looking directly at him with a warm smile, "that is what makes me laugh -- the pleasure of finally seeing openly what had hovered at the edges of my awareness."

Chapter 2

When he returned to the University the following afternoon, Bower told no one. He told no one of the cell in which he had spent the night, nor of the half a dozen others similarly incarcerated, not as prisoner but as torturer. It was not guilt that kept him from speaking. He did not feel guilty. He experienced the kind of exaltation being in love is reputed to induce. He was walking on air, and like a lover, understood implicitly that speech to anyone about the rituals of love could only dishonor them, especially when the rituals were such as he understood would bring shock and censure were they known. It would be called debauchery, at best, even by his open-minded acquaintances had they known the erotic ceremonies of Cruelty and Suffering that had become his spiritual nurture.

* * *

The Student Union was a masterpiece of deception. From outside it seemed to be a drunken and cockeyed, nevertheless perfectly balanced, edifice of mirroring glass. Inside, that glass was translucent and made anyone inside feel as if there were no boundary between the world outside and this protected space. The building's skin from within was a window forked by tough, curving, intersecting, tensile, supporting aluminum rods.

It was late in the afternoon. Martin's eyes were tired. He rubbed them as Elsa spoke. When vision came back to him, he turned and looked at the boy passing in the middle distance before them. Elsa felt his attention go. A blank space opened before her. It became impossible to make sense of anything. She forgot what she was saying.

Martin turned back to her. She appeared to blush. It was really anger, but she stifled it and rifled his hair.

To say that she had designs on Martin would be speaking accurately. Her parents would disapprove of him. But that was a big part of the attraction. She was rebellious and she was experimental in her rebellion. Her mother's disposition was starchy. She could tolerate no deviations from the way she thought the world ought to be. But Hanna

Blume had gotten under the girl's skin better than Elsa knew, and anyone who gave thought to the matter could see her acts of rebellion as nothing less than the clearest declarations of loyalty. She had entered a fight she wished to lose

"You're not here at all, are you?" she said bringing his head nearer her with the palm of her hand on his cheek.

He responded warmly when she kissed him and felt a frightening possibility of surrender.

"Let's go to my room," she said.

He consented. The day, because it was spring, had extended itself and as they walked in the late evening only the slightest suggestion of night was beginning to plant itself into the texture of the falling day. Across the campus they trod hand in hand with the liveliness of the young when they are imbued with the excitement of budding eroticism and the anticipation of its steep increase before they let burst together the great storm of joy.

He spread himself out above her and became a steely cloud and gently enveloped her in his mist as she dissolved in the moist warmth of their mutual rain. Afterwards he wished for a cigarette because he had engraved in his mind images in black and white from early French New Wave Cinema movies.

"You've changed over the last few weeks," she said looking up at him as he leaned on his right elbow, his entire body twisted somewhat to that side but not so much that he would become unplugged from her, and drew her to him.

"Oh, yeah," he said. "How?"

"In a good way," she said with empathic sincerity. "It's like you'd grown, like you've settled into yourself." She kissed him and he responded. The last sparks of their earlier explosion flared and spent themselves until after the shimmer of fading all feeling was gone but the utter joy of relaxation.

* * *

The top was up and Martin was protected from the downpour as he sped through the unusually dark evening over the dirt road beside what he had called the castle but later learned had been a monastery. He had settled into himself.

"You really intend to become a surgeon," Elsa said.

"Yes," he said.

"And when will you have time for me?" She was flirtatious and petulant and something else was lurking. He had to get away. It did not go on long. Martin told her one evening after classes that he was going to stop seeing her because her demands on him were too consuming and kept him from giving himself to his preparations to be a surgeon.

"You take the time we have," he said to her "and squander it, you ruin it, resenting the time we don't have rather than making the time we do have count for something."

She mocked his sentence but it did not matter. He left her. His heart was heavy -- for her. For himself, he was glad. His heart was light. He was free again of bondage to the conventions he had already managed several times to get free of. The curse of life was to be in other people's clutches.

Chapter 3

The wind was refreshing. His head needed to breathe. It was too long he had been holding on. Now he raced down the interstate until he came to the grass-edged dirt roads and took the one on the left through a forest until the meadow by the river where the monastery stood. The sky was drenched with stars. Inside, he sat at one of the long bars and drank a vodka martini. A jazz trio backed a singer going through parts of the Cole Porter Songbook. There were few members at the bar and most of the chambers on the second floor were not being used. But all of that was of no account. Richard walked in and for Martin a cloud lifted. He was tall and although thin, it was a muscular, compact thinness. His sandy blond hair caressed his skull and his head was balanced precisely upon the lean pillar of a strong neck. They kissed in greeting.

"I wanted to see you all week," Martin said, embracing him.

"I could not get you out of my mind."

"I'm hard for you all of the time."

"I want you now," Richard said and pressed his mouth to Martin's.

"Come," Martin said, pulling away. They swallowed the last of their drinks and took the rose marble steps to a chamber on the second floor where the balcony looks down at the fountain in the atrium. The room had been prepared for them.

"Come inside me, please," Richard said. "I am such a vulnerable slut when I am with you. You don't know how much I need you."

This unguarded confession of desire pierced Martin's own reserve and acted upon his nerves with an electricity that is un-representable by language although it is searing in the flesh. It was intolerable to feel. It was a clawing, craving demand on his flesh. He did not want to accede to it.

"Fuck off, faggott," he said.

Richard looked at him with dumbfounded amazement. "But you," he began, but before he could finish, Martin had slapped his mouth shut with a sharp crack on the cheek.

"You still want me inside you?" Martin said.

"Oh, yes," Richard affirmed nodding his head.

Bower pulled open his shirt and stood torso bare, broadcasting his impenetrable masculinity. He raised his chin and slowly turned his back on Richard, who had fallen to his knees. Bower walked out of the room onto the marble terrace outside. He leaned up against the marble parapet and looked down at the powerful spray shooting upwards in the fountain at the center of the atrium.

Richard could not cope with it. He felt a sudden emptying out of his belly. Inexpressible grief and despair overwhelmed him. "Martin," he cried. Bower walked back into the room and locked the door behind him. "It's not a game," he said. "It's a matter of power. I have it. You don't. That says something about you."

Richard did not like hearing what Martin was saying. He knew it was true and it made him numb. He wanted the power of words, tender that becalmed the spirit with abundance of affection.

"You'll sleep on the floor," Martin said, looking down at Richard and opening the door to admit the boy whom he had summoned when he stood at the parapet.

Take me into bed with you, please," Richard begged.

Martin ignored him. He was excited and like iron: he gazed at the boy: the more he frustrated Richard, the stronger he felt. He swelled with the pride of being unyielding. He held the boy and drilled him with kisses, oblivious to him as he possessed him. He let him go.

Richard stood immobile by the doorway, his gaze fixed on them; his heart, pricked by an icy knife, wept as it beat.

Martin left the boy and approached him.

Richard fell to his knees. Martin pushed him to the ground. When his lips were near Martin's feet, he stretched to kiss them, but Martin kicked him away. Richard curled up on the floor, lay still, unable to sleep, unable to move.

"Are you alright?" Martin asked Richard, the next morning, once he had sent his night's companion scooting out the door. He extended a hand to help him stand.

"A little bit sore," he said, bent.

"This will straighten you out," Martin said, taking hold of Richard's nipples and pinching them hard. It did.

Richard could hardly contain the gratitude he felt when Martin kissed him. Martin sensed it, but it did not infuriate him. It warmed him.

He felt tenderness toward the gentle soul he dominated. He was set up as a protector by the natural scheme of things. It could be a burden, but it could also be a joy. He kissed Richard warmly and left him for another time.

Chapter 4

The winter sun was strong and already suggested spring's approach. Elsa kept Martin in her sights despite his defection.

"Where do you go?" Elsa asked, as she walked up beside Martin, acting as if they were still a couple.

"Go?" Martin said.

"Yeah, when you go away for a weekend or a night."

"Into another world."

"What the hell does that mean?"

"Just what it says."

Elsa frowned at this evasion. "I want you to stay in this one," she said.

"I told you it was no go. I'm going to go into whatever world I want to."

"You want me to be a boy," she said knowingly, as if having unmasked him.

"I want you to get off my back."

"You don't know what you want. You don't know if you want a girl or a boy, and it's for sure you don't know how to make me feel like a woman."

"If that's true, what do you want from me?" he said, guiding them off the cobblestone path onto the grass and then standing beside an old, tall, spreading chestnut tree. He took her in his arms as if he were her father or her brother. "Look, I don't want to take anything away from you," he said, as if talking to a child, looking straight at her, "but I can't surrender myself to you either. Demanding that, you will only frustrate yourself even more."

She heard his words but let them slip past her. She felt his body outlining hers as he held her comfortingly. She sighed and looked up at him and he understood she wanted his mouth on hers and her breath flowing at his rhythm. He was moved by her need and desired it at that moment, too, but he knew that if he recognized and satisfied that need he would not subdue it but stimulate it. And then it would corner him, trap him. He held back and then he withdrew.

"What?" she said.

"I am only cruel to be kind," he said.

"You're full of shit," she said.

"It's getting dark," he said. "I'll take you to the edge of the park and then we can go our own ways."

"I don't need your help to walk across the campus," she said coldly, "even in the twilight."

"I know you don't," he smiled. "I'm going this way, then. Take care of yourself."

He left her in knots. She could not figure out if he was deliberately trying to or if he was just so incredibly stupid. But he was not stupid. She knew that. Her pain was that much deeper. It lasted for several months. The langor lasted with little abatement throughout the summer and the only thing that defeated hopelessness was the inexorability of routine.

He disappeared, or as good as had. Every now and then she spotted him at a distance and knew not to go near. She cursed herself for spotting him, dreading the grief it would bring to her day.

She learned in the fall that he had transferred. Some kind of fast track program that put him in medical school a year quicker. Whatever. He was gone. And she was glad. So was he. He was living with Richard, not quite as lovers, but with Richard in submission to him. It was very convenient. He began medical studies and was cared for, fed, soothed, stroked and adored by someone.

"It's not that you love me. I can tell you don't," Richard said, placing a mug of coffee on the counter in front of Martin. "You just like how it feels to have someone completely at your disposal, to take care of every need."

"Absolutely."

"I'm a convenience."

"You are a necessity," Martin said, lifting Richard's chin with his index finger and delicately biting his lips, as if tasting him. "Actually, a little bit of a luxury."

* * *

The hailstorm had come on unexpectedly; moments before there had been sunny skies. But ice pebbles came with a frightening force banging relentlessly on the windows. Martin stood, still without his shirt and barefoot although he had pulled his jeans back on.

"You don't need a new car," Richard said smiling, "for example. You over indulge yourself. You are just out of school. You've just gotten a job in the best hospital in New York."

"You don't know what I need," Martin said slowly, emphasizing each word with a slight squeeze of Richard's pointed nipples.

"Ok, what do you need it for?" Richard said, hardly able to think.

"I want it. Isn't that enough?"

"Is it?"

"You tell me."

"No, it is not."

Martin tilted his head to the left and jutted his jaw forward. "To each his own," he said.

"Aren't you ever satisfied?" Richard said.

"I'm always satisfied," he said. "You're the one who's continually frustrated."

"That's because you keep leading me on and then withdrawing."

"Poor Uncle Wiggly," Martin said, taking Richard's cock between his fingers pinching it and letting it go after a few searing frets and slides, drawing him near to the edge but pulling him back until he was dizzy.

"Take me there," Richard begged. Martin let go his cock and before he registered, cuffed Richard's wrists together behind his back. Richard froze immobilized, statuesque, surrendering to sensation as Martin ran his hands over his body and dug his fingers into his flesh and made him feel like he was sculpting him.

He stood back, gazed at him, took his jeans from off a nearby chair and got into them, pulled a polo shirt over his chest that showed it all the more, tongued Richard's lips and left him.

Elsa had not had an easy time. She had been burned by the anger her failed relationship with Martin aroused in her. She seethed when she remembered. The only thing, she imagined, that could satisfy her, would be if he could be made to recognize what he had done and if he could be made to repent it. She bit her teeth. She had no way of getting that. That's what the fall was, the beginning of consciousness. Memory becomes a torment and resentment becomes the dominating passion. He had unfastened himself from her. The best thing she could do, she knew it, was to get purged of it all – get it out of her mind and out of her system. That took will and concentration. For their triumph over regret and resentment, she knew, there had to be an object. She needed a discipline, something to concentrate on. It was the Law, with its precision, particularity, and especially with its dependence on ordered argument, that captivated her.

Upon graduating, she was lucky enough to land a job at the Morrison Agency, a firm specializing in public relations and celebrity damage control. She was sharp, incisive, and, when need be, ruthless. She rose from intern to associate in a matter of two years and after another three years to an executive position; she left Morrison to open her own office. She did not solicit any of the clients she had at Morrison to switch, but a number of her clients, hearing of her new venture, followed her, and her agency thrived.

She was often bored when not working. She began a relationship with Tom, a good-looking guy a few years younger than she was whom she had hired as her assistant. But the more she attached herself to him romantically, the less she became able to maintain her superior status with regard to him. Her sense of need humiliated her. She was stuck, and it was only after she discovered, before anything serious occurred, that he had begun doctoring invoices so that he could skim part of the fees off for himself that she dismissed him from her employ and her bed.

It was a transforming experience for her. "I've been a fool," she said, sitting in Bernie's Helicopter, the rooftop bar on Spring Street under a canopy of summer stars.

Marcia contradicted her, as friends will. But Elsa held her ground. "A fool."

* * *

"This looks interesting," Richard said as he handed Martin an invitation that had come in the mail inviting him to attend an interdisciplinary conference and moderate a panel on the varieties of dominant/submissive relationships. He accepted and they flew to Seattle.

* * *

"You don't mean what you say," a streaky blond woman with dark eyebrows, slim cheeks, and high cheekbones said to him.

The crowd around him had thinned out. Martin was collecting his papers and arranging them on the lectern, looking down, but as she spoke he glanced up at her.

"How can you tell?" Martin said with a smile and a glance at Richard.

The woman would not be put off with a question for an answer. She looked at him intently and he could see what he thought to be a degree of animosity. She was defying him to look at her. That drew his gaze despite himself to her. Each time their gazes met, however, he would not engage but withdrew his. His papers conveniently needed his attention and he turned to arranging them and slipping them into his leather shoulder bag.

"You think you're better than anyone else," she said casually, as if their conversation were genial.

"Excuse me," he said, astonished.

"I could destroy you if I wanted to," the woman said.

Now Martin looked at her, unwavering.

"Yes?" he said. And there was no doubt about either the power he commanded or his confidence in its depth.

She blinked and walked away.

"What was that about?" Richard said.

"I don't know, but a lot of that sort of thing is happening lately."

"It gets you on edge," Richard said.

"No," Martin said, thoughtful, "I seem to get people on edge."

The End

Here is a sample from another story you may enjoy:

GIDEON ELLIOT

TABOO EROTICA

HYPNOTIZED

3 IN 1 BOXED SET

I'D KNOWN Jason since we were kids. I've always admired him – so much that it sometimes overwhelmed me. My admiration began with the way he looked. I always just enjoyed seeing him. He was a scrawny kid at the pool in the summertime, but lithe. He was adorable. When I think of him now, as I remember him during the summer, many years ago, when we were both seven, I can still see him as we undressed in the bungalow our families shared in Rockaway. He looked, stretching himself out of his little wet speedo, like nothing so much as a plucked chicken.

In his early teens he was smart and snappy and thoughtful, dressed sharp, got into gym and working out, as well as folk music – he taught himself guitar -- film noir, the Marquis de Sade, differential calculus, Nietzsche, and automobile engines. Girls talked about him, giggling with desire. He was easy around them, affectionate, cuddly, and, although he dated, he never got tied down to one girl friend. But none of the girls he dated expected him to, and none of them lacked for dates with other guys.

What was really beautiful is that he allowed me to love him. He was glad to accept it; he didn't push me away. When I looked at him with wondering eyes, with helpless admiration, he just grabbed me by the shoulder and horsed around for a minute.

Then he'd smile in the friendliest way. I didn't feel the least bit ashamed for showing my devotion. I'm always at ease with him but there are moments when I feel the excitement shaking inside me like I do with no one else. He's noticed it. And he doesn't hold it against me.

He'd go nuts if he couldn't accept love, 'cause he's a guy that everybody's crazy about, and he even can stay friends with girls who are dying for him but he won't sleep with them.

***

WE WERE in Butler library. We were seventeen. It was after ten, and the place was relatively empty. I'd managed to read all of Mill's *On Liberty* and I was thinking about the various possible extents and limits of human responsibility. I didn't get anyplace solid in my thought. I was spacey, floating, feeling like I was thinking but unable, the next moment, to remember exactly what I had been thinking.

Suddenly I heard fingers snap in front of my face and I saw Jason grinning. He'd just finished an assignment in differential calculus. If I had just had to squeeze my brain into that mold for two hours, I would not have been smiling.

"Where are you, Buddy?"

"I'm thinking about the limits of social responsibility and how you determine how much control any person can put on another; or an abstract group, like society, on the individual."

"Did anyone ever tell you that you lose yer bloom when you think."

"Cut the shit," I said, laughing at how beautifully he could move me from one place to another without even noticing it. "Aren't you tired of calculus already?" I said. "You're thinking all the time, and you haven't lost your bloom."

"Let's get some coffee," he said, throwing his arm round my shoulders.

"And stay up all night?"

"Don't worry."

Well, when Jason says "don't worry," you don't worry.

I couldn't get enough of him. I suppressed my sexual desire in order to be able to keep being with him. He didn't mind how I felt, but still I didn't want to make him uncomfortable by putting him in the awkward position of feeling like demands were being made on him, or of seeming like he was rejecting me. Most of the time it worked. I forgot about how much I wanted him and just enjoyed being with him the way we were. I forgot my sexual desire, or maybe it lingered as a ground bass giving greater resonance to whatever we did. I had become like an anorexic. Something else was more important to me than eating.

If you enjoyed this sample then look for **Hypnotized**.

Also by this Author

A Second Chance

The Recruiter

A Furtive and Hidden Embrace

Diamond Shadows

Displacement

Keen Obedience

Between Two Thieves

Heart's Desire

Sensual Surrender

Erotic Aggression

Don't Forget You Love Me

Unstable Emotion

The Hazard Game

A Knight in the Forest

Captured Emotions

The Mesmerist's Tale

On His Own

The Good Bitch

Succumb Touch

Blue Identity

***

I REALLY LOVE Reviews!

If you enjoyed this book, please share the love and don't forget to leave a review on Amazon or the site of any other retailer you purchased this book from!

I highly appreciate your reviews, and it only takes a minute to write & post one. I can't tell you how much this means to me!

You'll find the list of all my books on my Author Central page... just in case you'd like to leave a review for other books of mine you've read but didn't have time to leave a review.

*Amazon Author Central – http://www.amazon.com/Gideon-Elliot/e/B00DUYBEQC

One Last Thing, For Kindle Readers...

When you turn the page, Kindle will give you the opportunity to rate this book and share your thoughts on Facebook and Twitter. If you enjoyed my writings, would you please take a few seconds to let your friends know about it? Because... when they enjoy they will be grateful to you and so will I.

Thank You!

Gideon Elliot
gideon_elliot@awesomeauthors.org

About the Author

Gideon Elliot was born in 1981 in Wichita, Kansas.

He grew up in San Francisco and spends the greater part of the year, now, on one of the Cyclades Islands in Greece where he runs a jazz café, paints, writes poetry, and swims.

He has a small apartment in Greenwich Village, where he stays from the middle of November to the end of April and, during those months, manages an erotic men's clothing shop. He began writing erotic fiction at the age of fifteen.

You may also like the books by these authors:

AMY REDEK

OUT IN THE
REAL
WORLD

GAY TRANSVESTITE EROTICA

'Why were you dressed as a woman when you were arrested?' the solicitor who had been assigned to me asked.

'I was on my way to work and stopped in the pub for a drink,' I replied.

'Work? Dressed as a woman? Why?'

That same old question, why. It cropped up many times before and yet there were still very few times that I could answer it. I gave out a sigh.

'I work in a transvestite night club as a female impersonator. Does that answer your question?' I asked.

'Not really. I would have thought that you would have been dressed in, ah, trousers and the like and changed when you got to work,' he said.

'I haven't any, ah, trousers and the like,' I said sarcastically. 'All of my wardrobe consists of women's clothes.'

'Why?'

'Oh for Christ's sake! Because I like dressing up as a woman!'

'Mr. Trent, or can I call you Jack?' he asked.

'Jackie. Everybody who knows me calls me by that name. I'm even billed under the name.'

'Okay. Jackie. I've been assigned by the court to defend you and so I must know something of your background and exactly what happened in that pub. The charge is affray, assault, damage to property, assaulting two police officers and resisting arrest as well as abusive language. How will you plead?'

'Not guilty, of course! I was only defending myself. She started it!' I said.

'But you put her into hospital as well as one of the police officers,' he said.

'Serves them both right. Her for starting it and him for grabbing me like he did, look!' I pulled up the torn sleeve of my dress and showed him the purple bruise marks on my upper arm, the imprints of fingers clearly to be seen. 'He shouldn't have gripped me so hard. I didn't know it was a copper when I swung round and hit him. I was only defending myself.'

'The other woman suffered a broken nose and cuts to her face from the glass you smashed into her face.' I gave a snort at this.

'Other woman my arse! That was Maurice Goodchild, also known as Maureen. A blowsy queen that shouldn't be out on the streets at her age.'

'Maurice Goodchild?' he asked, looking quite surprised at this news.

'Yes. I didn't know it was her tom I was chatting up while she was out in the cottages,' I said.

'Cottages?' he queried.

'Toilets to you,' I replied. 'He was sitting by himself and I thought he was good looking enough to have a chat with and so I sat down to talk. Next minute I was hit on the shoulder by Maureen who started screaming at me and she went and tore my sleeve so I hit her with my beer glass. I didn't know I had it in my hand, I thought I was using my fist. I know the glass broke in my hand and I could see blood coming from her nose but I wasn't going to give her a chance of hitting me back so I jumped on her.'

'Smashing two tables and a chair in the process,' my solicitor said.

'It was as much her fault as mine as well as her tom for he jumped on my back. It was him that caused us to crash into the other tables.'

'What's Tom's last name?' he asked. 'We may have to call him as a witness.'

'Tom?' I snorted. 'That's not his name! That's the name given to a man that picks up the likes of her. What his real name is I've no idea, I've never seen the man before.'

'Okay,' he said. 'So you started to chat him up, why?'

'Well if he was agreeable, we would have gone out to the cottages,' I said.

'Why?'

'What planet are you on? To have him fuck me, of course.'

'Oh! You mean you were actually soliciting then?'

'Am I being charged with that too?' I asked.

'No.'

'Then yes, I was. Isn't that what you do being a solicitor? Getting clients so that you can fuck them?' I asked with a smile.

'Not quite,' he said, having to laugh at the suggestion which made him almost human. 'That has already happened to them and we try to help them as best we can, like you.'

'I never got round to being fucked before the fight started,' I said.

'But you're fucked now unless I can get you off.'

**

As he said, he didn't get me off and so I was fucked. I was found guilty and sentenced to three months' prison. I don't suppose my turning up in court wearing a dress helped my case, but I was going to either win or go down with my colours nailed to the mast. My solicitor did the best he could but it was my kicking the second copper in the balls as I was being held that turned things against me.

I got a lot of sneers from the guards as I was dumped in Wandsworth Prison later that day. I won't go into all the names I was called by the guards in there as I had to strip off my clothes for a shower before being given my prison clothes to wear. I was escorted into C Block and up on the second tier, a cell door was opened and I was told to go in.

'Well bless me if it isn't Jackie Trent,' the lag on the upper bunk said as I went inside and heard the cell door clang behind me.

'Hallo Bert,' I said. 'Never thought that I'd meet you in here?' Bert Wilson was a pickpocket, though I think he was beginning to suffer from arthritis for he seemed to get caught more often now he was getting older. I knew him from the outside and he'd been into my club a few times.

'Why are you here?' he asked, sitting up and letting his legs dangle down.

'You know Maureen Goodchild?' I asked and he nodded. 'Well I gave her a new nose job and ruined a copper's love life, putting them both in hospital. They gave me three months.'

'Well this is going to upset your love life too then,' he chuckled.

'Not really for this is a men's prison and there must be quite a few who are quite randy. As I'm in here with you Bert, would you like to be the first?'

'I've got no money, Jackie,' he said a little disconcertedly.

'As we're going to be cell mates, it's free for you,' I said and saw his face light up in a smile which broadened even more as I stroked the front of his trousers and felt that he'd suddenly risen up.

'Oh Jackie,' he said as he slid off the top bunk and landed down next to me. 'Can I kiss you too?'

'Of course,' I said with a laugh as I undid my trouser buttons.

He grabbed me with his arms and gave me a good smacking kiss on the lips as I dropped my trousers and turned round and leaned down onto the lower bunk. Like me, he didn't give a hoot as to what the other cells on the other side of the block could see as I heard his trousers come down and felt the tip of his of erection press against my rear.

'Push in and fuck me, Bert. It's been two weeks since my last cock.'

I gave out a big sigh as I felt him push and enter my backside. It was lovely to have a cock back inside me again and I reveled in his movements as he shafted me, almost drooling as he held my hips firm as he fucked me. I think he might have been without anything like this for a long time for he was soon holding me tight as he came, bucking his hips. I felt his seed spatter my insides and welcomed the soothing massage he was giving me.

It was over too soon and I gave out a mew as he pulled out and staggered to the metal basin to wash his cock before putting it away. I'd pulled my trousers up and got onto the lower bunk and sighed at just having had a lovely fuck. When he'd finished, he turned and got onto the bunk with me and gave me a kiss.

'Thanks Jackie, you don't know how much I needed that,' he said as he kissed me again.

'Anytime, Bert, anytime. I'm not going anywhere for the next three months,' I said, reliving the pleasure of having a hard penis rouse my insides again. 'Who's the Baron?' I asked, that being the term for the prisoner who was the top dog of the place.

'Eddie Forbes,' he replied.

Bert didn't have to enlarge on that for I knew who Eddie Forbes was. He was a bank robber and was serving twelve years of which he'd already served four. I knew him by sight though not to talk to and I looked out for him when we went down to the mess hall for dinner. I queued up with the others for our supper and some was dumped on my metal tray and then looked for where this Eddie Forbes was sitting. I saw his table and walked over with my tray and though the table was full, I stopped by him.

'Can I sit down here?' I asked. There were some scowls from the others seated but not from Eddie. He looked me up and down and at least it was with frankness and not as if he was looking at a heap of shit.

'Certainly Jackie,' he said. 'Shift!' he demanded of the men that were sitting opposite him and so they started to shuffle their backsides along the bench and the guy at the end had to get up and with a scowl at me, moved onto another table as room was made for me opposite Eddie.

'So what does our catamite Jackie want of me?' he queried as I sat opposite him and began to eat from my tray. I smiled at him.

'Your cock and protection in either order,' I said, looking him in the eye. 'I'm willing to look after you if you'll look after me…'

If you enjoyed this sample then look for <u>Out In The Real World</u>.

My name is Sean Collins. I was just promoted to become the manager of the interior cabinet and counter top department of a huge Home Store. I started out working here in high school as a kid who did anything and everything and after two summers in high school and now two years more working full time I got promoted. My skills in customizing cabinets and working with homeowners to install them helped me get the job. Now I'm the boss and have two workers under me.

I'm not your typical construction worker. I'm only five foot eight and I weigh about a hundred and forty pounds. I'm not a muscle man but I'm fit. I guess you'd say I have a preppy look. I wear my brown hair in a messy-look style. I have blue eyes and I think I'm pretty decent looking.

My social life is sadly lacking. I've never had a girlfriend and since I moved to this town I've never really made a lot of new friends. Oh sure, I have buddies at work but none of them know the real me. I'm gay. No one knows and I want to keep it that way.

I have a small apartment just a few blocks from the store and drive a Buick. I know, that's an old man's car but it's a damn nice car and I love it. I like my work and hope that eventually I'll get the guts to make a move on somebody who is gay like me and find a boyfriend. Until then, I jack off a lot.

One of the guys who worked in my department got married and moved to another city, so today I'm meeting his replacement. I hated to see the other guy go because he was a hell of a good worker. I hope this new guy will work out.

I got a call from the manager telling me my new guy was in his office, so I went to meet him and take him back to our department. When I walked in I got a little twitch in my dick. Damn he was gorgeous.

"Sean, this is Taylor Fox," the manager said.

I looked at the guy as he stood up. He looked like he was my age, 21, or a little older. He was a big strapping six-foot tall guy and looked like he weighed about one eighty. He was wearing work boots, jeans and a tank top. His shoulders and arms were very well muscled and his chest was beautiful. He was wearing a baseball cap but under it there was medium-length brown curly hair sticking out the sides.

His face was beautiful. He had amazing pale blue eyes and a flawless face with perfect white teeth and a very nice smile. He was a fucking hottie from the word go.

"Taylor," I said. "Nice to meet you."

"Mah pleasure," he said.

I looked at the manager.

"Taylor recently moved here from Missouri," he said smiling. "He worked at a Home Store there for a couple of years."

"Oh great, so you have experience," I said.

"Ah know which end of a hammer to hang onto and Ah've got all mah fingers."

He grinned. Damn he was handsome.

"Well that's a start for sure."

I took him to the storeroom to get him some uniform shirts. We all wear red golf shirts with gold lettering on them and a nametag on the pocket.

"Are you a large or extra large?"

He pulled off his tank top. I know my mouth dropped open. His chest was beautiful from his hard pectorals to his dark little nipples. He had a very pronounced six-pack and his belly was hard and tapered to a pronounced V as it disappeared into the top of his jeans. He had a thin gold chain around his neck with a small gold cross hanging at the bottom of it. His skin was tan and perfect. The jeans were riding low on his hipbones and there was a line of pubic hair sticking out of the top. He turned to put his shirt on the table and an inch of his butt crack was showing above the top of his jeans.

"Let me try a large," he said.

I handed him the shirt. He pulled it over his head revealing a thick thatch of brown hair under his arms. The shirt fit but was a little tight.

"Maybe an extra large?" I asked.

"Ah like this one. Ah like my shirts tight."

"You have all the right stuff to fill them out," I thought but didn't say it.

I went to the shirt box and got him five more shirts. Each employee got half a dozen so they could wear a clean one every day and have a spare. Then I went to the secretary and told her his name and to make him a name badge.

"They don't allow caps at work," I said.

"Sorry. Ah'll put it someplace."

"We each have a locker," I said. I took him to the break room and gave him a locker. He put his tank top and cap in the locker.

"Well, let's go to the cabinet shop and I'll give you the grand tour."

"Were you in the cabinet shop where you worked before?" I asked as we walked back to my area.

"Ah sold paint. But Ah'm pretty handy."

"I'm sure you'll do just fine. How old are you?"

"Just turned 21," he said.

"Married?"

"Oh hell no. Ah had me a girlfriend bout a year ago. Ah made the mistake of movin in with her. Oh man, that was a mistake. Nag nag nag. No amount of pussy was worth that, and to tell the truth, she was a piss poor fuck anyway."

That was a bit more information that I'd expected. But I got the point. He was straight.

"Ya'll married?" he asked.

"No."

"Girlfriend?"

"No."

Since I didn't volunteer any more information, he let it drop.

I showed him our area and he seemed like he was pretty comfortable with the tools and other stuff. I customer walked up and I talked to them about what they were looking for. Taylor listened and watched. Then another guy walked up.

"Ah'll go see if'n Ah can help him," he said.

That impressed me. He wasn't afraid to step up.

We both finished about the same time. I had a tentative cabinet job for the kitchen of a new house. Taylor gave his customer a form to fill out the dimensions of a bathroom layout. We'd both done well.

"You did well. You don't seem to be bashful," I said.

"Oh hell no. Ah like people and helping them."

We worked for the next couple of hours and then it was lunchtime. The other guy in our department is an older guy who is a hell of a cabinetmaker named Joe. He and Taylor got along real well too. Joe said he'd hold down the fort while we got lunch.

"Where do ya'll eat?" Taylor asked.

"There are three places in this mall. There's a Taco Bell, Wendy's and KFC."

"Kenfucky Tried Chicken," Taylor said grinning.

"The Colonel will haunt you," I said.

"What ya'll hungry for?"

"I'm good for any of them."

"Let's git some tacos."

We went to Taco Bell and both got a burrito. We sat in a booth. Taylor was very animated and fun to talk to. I loved watching him talk. He was so damn good-looking that some of his stories, even though they were a bit silly, seemed fun to listen to. He was a country boy through and through. He told me of some of his exploits with his buddies and it didn't seem he was afraid to try anything. I really liked him from the start.

We finished and went back to work. At the end of the day we clocked out and walked to the parking lot.

"What d'yall do around here?" he asked.

"Oh most nights I just go home. Sometimes I stop for a beer. On weekends I go fishing sometimes."

"Ya'll got a lake around here?"

"We have a nice river. You can catch bass and walleye and catfish."

"Damn, Ah like to fish. Maybe we can go sometime."

"Hell yeah. How about this coming weekend? I don't have anything planned."

"Sounds good to me."

We got to a nice four-wheel drive pickup.

"This here is ma ride."

"Wow, it's nice," I said.

"Where's yours?"

I hated to show him. I pointed to the Buick. It was an older model and a Park Avenue. It's a big luxury car.

"Oh," he said.

I laughed.

"I know, it's a grandpa car but the damn thing is so nice to drive. If I get in a wreck I'll be as safe as hell."

"Yeah, I guess so. But if we fishin we'll take mine."

He grinned at me. He opened the door and put his extra shirts on the seat. Then he stripped off his shirt he'd been wearing and put his baseball cap on his head. He climbed up into the cab and about an inch of his butt crack was showing.

"See ya'll in the morning Sean," he said.

He started the truck and grinned as he pulled away. I walked to my car with his damn good-looking face and perfect body in my mind. I rubbed my cock. His butt crack flashed into my memory. My cock was getting hard.

"Oh boy, I'm gonna have a sweet jack off tonight."

I stopped and picked up a pizza for dinner. I kicked off my sneakers when I walked into my apartment. I put the pizza on the kitchen countertop and went to the bedroom and took off my clothes except for my boxers. I scratched my balls and then pissed, washed my hands and went to the refrigerator and got a beer. I put two slices of pizza on a plate, grabbed a piece of paper towel for a napkin and sat on the couch and turned on the TV.

I put my feet up on the coffee table and ate my pizza and drank my beer. I didn't get much out of the TV. I was thinking of Taylor and how hot he was. I knew I was wasting my time but it sure was nice to have someone like him to work with. If I couldn't touch, at least I could look.

The more I thought about it the hornier I got. Eventually I had a hard on and pulled it out of the piss slit of my boxers. I wrapped my hand around it.

"Too bad you don't get more work," I said to my cock. My hand ran up and down my six-inch shaft and I played with my balls with the other hand. I closed my eyes and pictured Taylor with his shirt off. Damn I'd like to suck his nipples.

I wondered what his cock looked like. I pictured it being perfect like the rest of him.

My cock began to tingle and I squirted cum up on my belly. My cock dribbled on my boxers. I milked it out and then took off my boxers and wiped up. I tossed them in my hamper and got into the shower.

I stood under the warm water. Damn I wished I had a boyfriend. It would be so nice to come home to someone and be able to have sex and cuddle. I wondered if I'd ever find a guy. I had my doubts.

Taylor was already in our department when I got to work. He was looking at some kitchen plans that had been left by a homeowner.

"How was your evening?" I asked.

"Not too exciting. Ah'm living in a rented room in a house that an old lady owns. She lives there too. Ah have a bedroom and can use the kitchen."

"Why are you living in a place like that?"

"Well Ah wasn't sure this job would work out so Ah found a place that was cheap just in case."

"So do you think it will work?"

"So far Ah think Ah'm going to like it here. Joe is a real nice guy."

I expected him to say something nice about me.

"Yeah he is," I said.

Then he grinned.

"And my boss is pretty cool too," he said.

"Thanks, I think we'll get along fine. I stopped at the office and there is a small installation job that needs to be done. I usually take Joe along because he's a hell of a carpenter but this is just one overhead cabinet in a bathroom and a vanity and marble top. I'm going to take you along so we can see how we work together."

"Yer takin me? Cool."

We loaded up the material and took one of the vans that the store owned. The house was on the other side of town.

"So ennything happening this weekend?" he asked.

"I have no plans."

"Want to do something?"

Wow. He asked me to spend time with him. Oh man.

"Sure. What do you have in mind?"

"Somethin outside."

"Well we talked about fishing, I'd like to go down to the river and fish."

"Cool, but Ah don't got a pole."

"I've got plenty. We can take a cooler with a few beers and something to eat and make a day of it."

"Sounds like a plan Boss."

We got to the house and carried the two cabinets and marble top in. We measured and marked the wall and installed the upper cabinet. One of us had to hold it while the other put a few screws in to hold it. Taylor held it up and I got one screw in and then had to reach under him to get the other in. His shirt slid up as he held the cabinet up on the wall and I was right up against him trying to get to a place where there was something to screw into. My face was right by his crotch and I could see his pubes sticking up out of his jeans.

"Holy fuck,"

If you enjoyed this sample then look for **Seducing A Redneck**.

PURE GAY OBSESSIONS

RED HOT CONFESSIONS

A
COMPILATION
Hot Gay Erotica

Dick Clinton

I slipped from the table, onto the floor and knelt in front of my man fucker. He seemed dismayed that I wanted to make love to him, but just as soon as I was on my knees, I found the beauty that he possessed between his legs. I must admit his cock took me aback. It wasn't completely hard, and hung down almost to his knee. He was partially circumcised but had just enough foreskin to cover part of his cock head while soft. I started kissing his cock while I reached for his equally large balls. I looked up at Coach and smiled then took his semi-soft cock into my mouth and sucked it in as far as I could before I gagged. I was already experienced enough to take my foster dad's eleven-inch cock almost all the way down my throat and when it was flexible and soft, I could take it all.

I continued sucking Coach's cock until I had most of it down my throat. Coach let out a deep moan and looked down at me in amazement. It started to get harder and I had to back off. His cock was thicker than any cock I had ever perceived. It was as large around as a coke can or even larger. I was determined to suck him until he was about ready to cum, then I would show him I could take his cock into my asshole. I knew right then he must have a good 12 or even 13 inches of man cock. Wow. It was a beauty too. This man should be a male model for some magazines or even a 'cock stud' in adult movies. I would be willing to be his co-star anytime, that is, if I could manage to get it in me today.

Here I was on the floor, on my knees sucking my coach's big beautiful cock. I knew this one would be a challenge for me to take up my ass but I was determined to please the coach. I knew he was a gentle man and wouldn't do anything to harm me. I kept on sucking and making love to his cock until it was hard enough that I could not suck it all the way down my throat anymore. Now came the big challenge.

I looked up at coach to see a pleasant expression on his face. As I sucked him I knew I could get him off this way, but I knew it would be better if I let him fuck me while we were both this horny. I stood and rubbed his hairy chest and gently caressed one of his nipples while my other hand held firmly on his cock.

"Shall we give it a sporting try?" I said in jest as I got back up on the padded table, adjusted the height so he could get between my legs and guide his manhood deep into my willing asshole. He turned around to me as I placed my legs on his shoulders one at a time. He was still standing on the floor, his cock ass-level with my body. He smiled at me and placed some of the lube on the head of his cock and some on the entrance of my anus. It had some pain killing ointment mixed in with it so we could get started without much pain. I just hoped it didn't kill all the sensation of his cock. I wanted him to feel everything titillating.

He guided his manhood to my asshole and within a few seconds, the head of his penis had entered the first opening. He looked into my eyes to see if I was okay, then he moved in very slow and paused again. I bravely reached behind his firm, hard buttocks and moved his body into mine…

If you enjoyed this sample then look for **Pure Gay Obsessions**.

CHRIS JOHNS

MORE THAN A FRIEND

BDSM GAY EROTICA

Might as well do as I'm asked; I need a shower anyway, was the thought that ran through Matt's head as he sniffed his armpits.

Fifteen minutes later Alexander was back.

"Come with me," was all he said.

"But I have no clothes."

"You won't need them."

"But—"

"No buts, boy; do as you are told and come with me."

Feeling extremely embarrassed, Matt did as he was told. He had to find out what was going on, and the only way he could think to do that was to talk to the man by the pool.

Matt was nineteen and guessed the man on the sun bed to be about ten years older. As he approached, keeping a little behind Alexander, Matt noted the man, as he stood up, was probably an inch or two taller than him, well put together, without being over muscled. He couldn't see the eyes, which were covered with a pair of designer sun glasses, but noted the mid brown hair and the aquiline features, the golden tan with a dusting of hair on the chest, and, finally, the very pronounced bulge in his Speedos. He wasn't quite sure why his brain noted that fact particularly; men had never held his interest; women hadn't either, but he thought that being spaced out on drugs so often had put his sexual desires to sleep.

He stopped in front of the man and started to speak, but the man put a finger to his lips and stood in front of him.

"Listen, Matt, and learn. You will speak when spoken to, and you will obey every order given to you by me or my staff."

Matt interrupted, "Who the fuck are you?"

It was definitely the wrong thing to say. The man nodded, and before Matt could react, Alexander had him bent over a poolside table and delivered ten very hard slaps with his hand to Matt's bare arse.

Alexander was probably about six feet six inches tall, and around 225 pounds of what looked like solid muscle. A spanking from those hands was not something to want twice. Matt was howling when he was again stood facing the man, tears streaming down his face.

"As I was saying, you will call me Master at all times, and Alexander you will address as Sir. If you wish to speak, other than to answer a question, you will ask, 'Permission to speak, Master, or Sir', and wait to be given permission before continuing. If you utter any more profanities, you will be punished. Do you understand those instructions?"

Matt felt resentful, and made his second mistake.

"Yes," he mumbled.

Alexander was on him in a flash, delivering another very hard swat to his already very red ass. Matt yelped and jumped forward, almost knocking the Master over.

"Yes, what, Matt?" The man barked out.

"Yes, Master," was the now much more precise reply.

"Good. Now then, we are going to start cleaning you up before trying to turn you back into a civilised human being, inside as well. When I am finished, you will go with Alex. All of those disgusting bits of metal on you will be removed, and you will be given a respectable haircut. Then you can rejoin me for lunch. Tomorrow, you will be taken to a hospital for plastic surgery to restore your ear lobes to their proper shape. The following day, you will undergo laser treatment to remove all those tattoos, and then we will be left with a human being on the outside, instead of some painted and pierced animal. We will then spend however long we have to, training you to return to society as a useful and civilized person. Do you understand?"

Matt was fuming! "You can't do that! Let me go! You have no right to do this!" He was almost beside himself with anger, but not for long. Alexander was on him again and delivered another ten very hard slaps to a pair of cheeks already showing bruising from the first ten. Stood in front of the Master again, Matt was informed that there would be no more bare hand spankings.

"If you need chastising again, Matt, it will be with a cane. Do you understand?"

Through his sobs, Matt replied with a shaking voice, "Yes, Master."

If you enjoyed this sample then look for **More Than A Friend**.

Gay Romance Erotica

MASTERED

SENSUAL TALES FROM ANCIENT EGYPT

DEXTER CHASE

The Egyptians were rampant, raiding across the middle sea, raping and pillaging, but worst of all taking many slaves.It was always the youngest and most nubile of females and the prepubescent and middle teen boys. Those chosen were taken as sex slaves, to be used for their masters own sexual satisfaction and at times to be shared by other masters and forced to take part in orgies. The orgies that would make the later Roman ones pale into insignificance. I knew about the Roman orgies because that Empire grew as I too grew up, and I would eventually be taken there as an overseer for all the younger slaves that were taken from Egypt. Slaves in Egypt were invariably naked and most of the large houses had a bevy of young male and female slaves kept almost entirely for sex.

It was into one of these great houses that I was taken after being captured in one of the raids. I, too became one of those slaves all those years ago. I had passed into puberty and grown into a quite imposing youth at eighteen at the time I was captured. My new master was probably no older than thirty five but already he had a son my own age and several younger ones. He was a high ranking soldier and as one would expect he had a magnificent body. Before I became a slave, I had been mentored by a friend of my father's after puberty so I was well practiced in the art of man to man sex, us Greeks were not at all conscious that men having sex with boys was anything abnormal. The Egyptians didn't think like that so I was quite surprised that my master would fuck me frequently but I noticed he never allowed other men to fuck his eldest son. The eldest son was called Ptolemy, at eighteen he was almost too pretty to be a boy, made more so by the makeup he used on his eyes. I think I started to fall in love with him from the first day I saw him. He was always beautifully dressed and wandered around the villa with seemingly nothing to do. He would watch me work sometimes when his father was away and as I started to learn his language, he started talking to me.

By the time I was twenty his father had rather lost interest in me so I was trained to look after Ptolomy, his clothes all had to be perfect and ready to use at any time. The first time I left some of his clothes out instead of carefully putting them away I found that he was very strong and could be quite wicked.

"Ajax, how dare you leave my clothes like this?"

I realised he was very angry and fell to my knees begging his forgiveness.

"Of course I'm going to forgive you, after I have punished you. Come."

I knew where we were going. I had been to the punishment room before whenever I had displeased my master. I resigned myself to receiving a huge tranche of pain as I was whipped and knew that I would probably be in bed for a week unable to recline on my back. I was surprised at what happened, it was the first time that I had not been permanently marked. The slave master must have been an expert. A huge amount of debilitating pain but the skin hadn't been broked so I was not scarred.

"You have to learn that my clothes must always be perfect Ajax. What do you think would be an appropriate punishment for your dereliction of duty?"

He was being very imperious, but his manner made him appear very sexy and my wayward cock showed my arousal very quickly. It was very hard by the time Ptolomy had finished talking to me. The look on his face made me realise he had not seen my penis erect before. I didn't consider it to be huge, but it was certainly quite impressive. The master had enjoyed playing with it sometimes, but mostly he would just take me on his couch and fuck me quickly for mere satisfaction, he never made love to me. I think he found it easier to have the sex he wanted without all the complications of pregnancy and when he wanted to make love, he would take his wife. So different to my life in Athens. My mentor showed me how joyous lovemaking between males could be, my father had picked well and I knew when my time came I would make my wife happy and mentor the son of a friend when I was older. At that moment , I had no idea what would happen to me. I supposed that if I was less comely I would be sent to one of the work gangs building the pyramid to house the next pharaoh to die and I would be worked to death.

If you enjoyed this sample then look for **Mastered**.

WANT FREE COPIES OF MY BOOKS?

Just visit my blog and download free copies of my books:
http://gideon-elliot.awesomeauthors.org/gideon-elliot/